MW01385140

SALINA LIBRARY
100 BELMONT STREET
MATTYDALE, NY 13211
315-454-4524

SETTING LIMITS

BY STEPHANIE FINNE

BLUE OWL
BOOKS

TIPS FOR CAREGIVERS

Social and emotional learning (SEL) helps children manage emotions, learn how to feel empathy, create and achieve goals, and make good decisions. Strong lessons and support in SEL will help children establish positive habits in communication, cooperation, and decision-making. By incorporating SEL in early reading, children will be better equipped to build confidence and foster positive peer networks.

BEFORE READING

Talk to the reader about limits. Explain that they are boundaries and that everyone should have them.

Discuss: What are some limits that are already in your life? How do these limits keep you safe?

AFTER READING

Talk to the reader about how he or she can set personal limits. Explain that it is not always easy to do.

Discuss: What limits are important to you? How can you state your limits with respect? What will you do when someone doesn't respect your boundaries?

SEL GOAL

Some students may struggle with self-awareness, making it hard for them to learn and act on self-respect. Help readers develop self-awareness skills. Help them learn to stop, think, and talk about their feelings. How can they manage their needs? What do they need to feel respected? How can they stand up for their limits? Discuss how learning to do these things can help them set limits.

TABLE OF CONTENTS

CHAPTER 1
What Are Limits? 4

CHAPTER 2
Types of Limits 8

CHAPTER 3
Set Your Own Limits 16

GOALS AND TOOLS
Grow with Goals 22
Try This! 22
Glossary 23
To Learn More 23
Index 24

WHAT ARE LIMITS?

Can you eat candy for dinner? Can you yell at your teacher? No! These are limits set by adults.

Limits, or **boundaries**, are rules that are made to keep you safe. It is important to set limits for yourself, too. Why? Limits keep your mind and body healthy. They keep you **mindful** of what makes you feel safe and happy.

Setting boundaries helps you become **self-aware**. When you learn about yourself, you learn to respect your own limits. This is **self-respect**.

Part of being self-aware is knowing when and how to care for your body. This includes keeping your body clean. It also includes fueling your body with foods that are good for you.

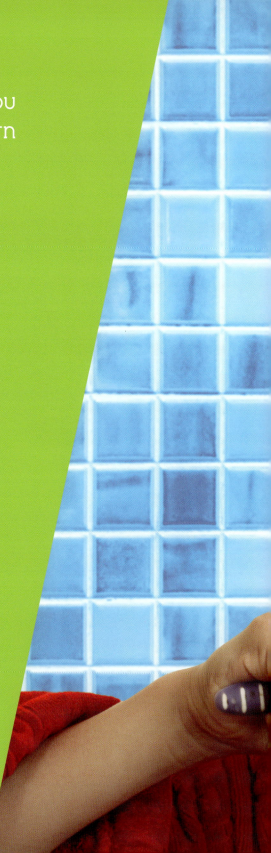

CHAPTER 2

TYPES OF LIMITS

There are five types of limits. **Material** limits are about belongings. Henry limits what he brings to school. He leaves his favorite toys at home. Why? This limit keeps his **property** safe.

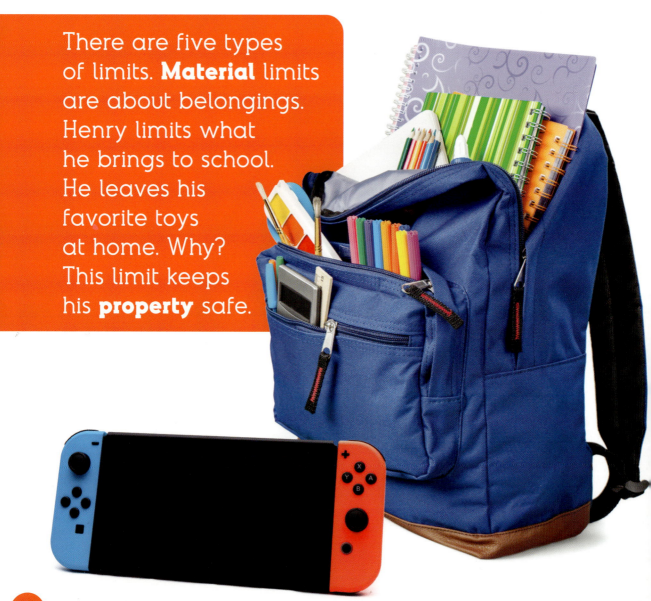

Physical limits involve **personal space**. Anna doesn't like to hug. She tells her uncle she isn't comfortable hugging. She offers a high five instead.

Healthy **mental** limits respect ideas. This includes respecting your own thoughts and **opinions**. Ella is being pressured to bully the new kid at school. She knows bullying is wrong. She sets a boundary. She decides that she won't give in to **peer pressure**. She will stand up for what she believes.

BUILD CONFIDENCE

Limits help you build **confidence** in your opinions. They determine how people behave around you. They also determine how you will respond when someone doesn't respect your limits.

Everyone is responsible for his or her own feelings. **Emotional** limits protect feelings. Ethan's dad has a new friend. Ethan doesn't feel comfortable sharing everything about himself with her. He decides to respect his emotional boundaries. How? He shares his feelings only when he is comfortable.

RESPECT

Respect is needed for limits to work. You must respect yourself and your limits. You must also respect others' limits.

There are also time limits. These can be for people or tasks. Too much time spent watching TV or playing video games can be bad for your body and mind. Setting time limits will help you put down devices. This gives you time for schoolwork or other tasks you need to do.

PRIORITIES

What are your **priorities**? Make a list. Knowing what is important to you will help you figure out what to spend more time on.

CHAPTER 3

SET YOUR OWN LIMITS

Now you know the kinds of limits. Let's work on setting one! The first step is to **identify** limits you already have. Maybe your family has a rule that you don't cheat when you play games.

The second step is to decide what limit you will set. Let's say you decide you don't want any lies in your friendships. Tell your friends your boundary. Make a mindful decision to start right away.

If a friend is lying, stop him or her firmly. Do this third step with just a few words. You can say, "Stop. I know you are lying."

Next, have an honest conversation with that friend. Talk about your boundaries. Talk about what you need. Do not argue. Do not say sorry for your limit.

Step five is to set a **consequence**. What if your friend lies to you again? You could set a limit to spend less time with that person. Be clear with your friend about what happens when your boundary is not respected. You must be willing to follow through with it.

Setting limits can be difficult. It takes practice. But everyone has a right to set his or her own limits. What limits will you set for yourself?

GOALS AND TOOLS

GROW WITH GOALS

Setting limits takes practice. Start by working on these goals.

Goal: Talk about boundaries with close friends and family. Find out what limits other people have.

Goal: Write down the limits that are already in your life. Then write down limits you would like to set. How can you put them into motion?

Goal: Practice setting limits. Role-play with an adult you trust to practice respectfully telling someone your boundary.

TRY THIS!

The best way to get good at something is practice! Role-playing is like putting on a skit to practice saying or doing something. Write a script for your boundary. You can make up characters and situations. You can even put on costumes or use puppets. The main goals are to get used to saying what your boundaries are and to practice what you will do when someone doesn't respect them. An adult can help you role-play different responses.

GLOSSARY

boundaries
Limits of something or certain behaviors.

confidence
Belief in your own abilities.

consequence
The result of an action, condition, or decision.

emotional
Of or having to do with feelings.

identify
To recognize or tell what something or who someone is.

material
Of or having to do with possessions.

mental
Having to do with or done in the mind.

mindful
A mentality achieved by focusing on the present moment and calmly recognizing and accepting your feelings, thoughts, and sensations.

opinions
Personal feelings or beliefs.

peer pressure
A feeling that you must do what other people of your age and social group are doing in order for them to like you.

personal space
The physical space immediately surrounding someone.

priorities
Things that are more important or more urgent than other things.

property
Anything that is owned by an individual.

self-aware
Able to recognize your own emotions and behaviors.

self-respect
Pride and confidence in yourself and your abilities.

TO LEARN MORE

Finding more information is as easy as 1, 2, 3.

1. Go to www.factsurfer.com

2. Enter "**settinglimits**" into the search box.

3. Choose your book to see a list of websites.

INDEX

behave 10

body 5, 6, 14

boundaries 5, 6, 10, 13, 17, 19, 20

confidence 10

consequence 20

decision 17

emotional limits 13

feelings 13

material limits 8

mental limits 10

mind 5, 14

mindful 5, 17

opinions 10

peer pressure 10

personal space 9

priorities 14

respect 6, 10, 13, 20

rules 5, 16

safe 5, 8

self-aware 6

self-respect 6

tasks 14

time limits 14

words 19

Blue Owl Books are published by Jump!, 5357 Penn Avenue South, Minneapolis, MN 55419, www.jumplibrary.com

Copyright © 2021 Jump! International copyright reserved in all countries. No part of this book may be reproduced in any form without written permission from the publisher.

Library of Congress Cataloging-in-Publication Data

Names: Finne, Stephanie, author.
Title: Setting limits / by Stephanie Finne.
Description: Minneapolis: Jump!, Inc., 2021 | Series: The sky's the limit | Includes index. | Audience: Grades 2–3
Identifiers: LCCN 2020036290 (print) | LCCN 2020036291 (ebook)
ISBN 9781645278610 (hardcover)
ISBN 9781645278627 (paperback)
ISBN 9781645278634 (ebook)
Subjects: LCSH: Time management–Juvenile literature. | Awareness–Juvenile literature. | Emotions in children–Juvenile literature.
Classification: LCC BF637.T5 F56 2021 (print) | LCC BF637.T5 (ebook) | DDC 155.4/19–dc23
LC record available at https://lccn.loc.gov/2020036290
LC ebook record available at https://lccn.loc.gov/2020036291

Editor: Jenna Gleisner
Designer: Anna Peterson

Photo Credits: Shutterstock, cover, 8; cglade/iStock, 1; Kostsov/Shutterstock, 3; Monkey Business Images/Shutterstock, 4; wavebreakmedia/Shutterstock, 5; Gravicapa/iStock, 6–7; Dreamstime, 9; Figure8Photos/iStock, 10–11; Iakov Filimonov/Shutterstock, 12–13; AVAVA/Shutterstock, 14–15; bonniej/iStock, 16; Kathy Quirk-Syvertsen/Getty, 17; Veja/Shutterstock, 18–19; Lopolo/Shutterstock, 20–21.

Printed in the United States of America at Corporate Graphics in North Mankato, Minnesota.